This book belong to

Your name:

THE GOLDEN PEACOCK

By: S Adler

Illustrations: Abira Das

English: Rivka Strauss

Just to say "Thank you" for purchasing this book,
I want to give you a FREE gift,
A Flip-Book for your kid.
At the end of this book.

Thank you so much

Sigal Adler

Long, long ago and far, far away,

A big pirate ship set sail one day,

It carried heavy sacks of silver and gold,

And three wicked pirates, strong and bold.

The pirates sang: "We stole from everyone,

Now we are the richest, our job is nearly done."

The people who'd been robbed could only cry,

They needed to think of something else to try.

So they went to visit the kind wizard, their friend:

He was old and wise and would help in the end.

When they told him about the pirates, a tale of woe,

He checked the spell book he'd had since long ago.

Flipping through the book, he didn't need to look far,

He read about a magic peacock who lived on a star.

This peacock sang special songs when it flew,

Tunes that defeated evil, and wicked pirates too.

The old wizard whistled and gazed into the sky,

Wings were flapping, coming down from up high.

The peacock had come; what a beautiful sight!

His regal golden tail feathers sparkled in the light.

The peacock flew over the pirate ship at sea,

He saw the men singing and dancing with glee.

Then he started humming his own special song,

The ship started to shake as it bumped along.

Now the sea was heaving and getting quite rough,

Waves rose up from the deep, but not yet enough.

The peacock kept on singing his beautiful song,

But the pirates felt sick; something was wrong.

Soaked by the waves, they shivered from cold,

One pirate felt drunk; his behavior was bold.

He took off his pants and then took off his shirt,

Jumped into the sea and disappeared with a squirt.

Two men on the ship knew they had to stay,

Guarding all their treasure was sure to pay.

They held on to their riches with all their might,

The singing didn't stop, but they held on tight.

The song got louder and brought the pirates to tears,

One let go of the rail so that he could plug his ears.

A great big wave blown onto the ship by the gale,

Threw him straight into the sea right over the rail.

Now one wicked pirate remained on the ship,

As it rolled with the waves; it was ready to tip.

He was a strong pirate; not afraid of the cold,

Nothing would make him give up his gold.

One pirate protecting his treasure all along,

One beautiful peacock with a magical song.

One thieving pirate who would never give in,

One magical peacock knew that he would win.

The peacock changed his tune to a different key,

Many sharp finned fish jumped out of the sea.

They poked the wicked pirate; attacked from every side,

Till he jumped into the sea and rode away with the tide.

The pirates never came back after that stormy day,

All the treasures were returned; the peacock flew away.

But the legend lives on and the story is often told,

About the pirates who were defeated by feathers of gold.

We are very happy that you read our story

This book was written With lots of love to all my readers.

Please Leave A Review on this Book Here

http://goo.gl/wukhN8

Thank you
Sigal Adler

Please Join My Free Mailing List

And Get A Free flipbook

www.sigaladlerbooks.com

FUN N SUN

41930390R10021

Made in the USA
Middletown, DE
26 March 2017